The Adventures of ECHO BOY and ABC Girl™

Created and Written By Chante Douglas

To my son who gave me my purpose in life and has made me the person I was destined to be. I love you.

Contact at: phillyaries82@gmail.com
Instagram: @autism_momma82

MW00995068

This story begins with a boy, but not just any boy. His name is Levi and when he uses his magic fidget spinner he transforms into ECHO BOY!

Here's how it all began...

One day he and his best friend Jasmine decided to go play at the playground. Jasmine really likes hanging out with Levi because they seem to understand each other. A real special connection.

The reason is because they both have Autism. Autism is a developmental disorder that impairs the ability to communicate and interact. Communication with Levi can be tricky sometimes because he has a speech disorder called Echolalia.
Echolalia is a repetitive speech like an echo.

As they arrive to the playground Jasmine finds a glitter crayon that catches her eye. As she leans down to grab it, in a blink of an eye she instantly transforms into ABC Girl!

Levi didn't really pay any attention to what was going on with Jasmine.
He was too busy swinging on the swings.
After he was done, he decided to get on the big twisting slide.

As he was climbing the steps, he found a fidget spinner.
He immediately picked it up and spinned it 6 times.
All of a sudden he transformed into ECHO BOY!

"WOW my super powers!" exclaimed Levi as he touched his cape.

He goes to find Jasmine and finds a girl dressed up like him except she's wearing a mask.
"Jasmine?" Levi asked.

"Hey Levi! Isn't this the coolest thing ever?" said Jasmine.
"Coolest thing ever!!!" said Levi.

"WOW Levi. even your shoes light up!"

"It's BLUUUUUUEEE! Hahahahaha!"
laughed Levi.
Levi starts running around the playground
because he loves the sound of the wind
hitting his cape.

Meanwhile, Jasmine practices using her
sparkle magic crayon, she writes the
letter "A" and POOF!!!!
...an apple appears!
"APPLE!!!" said Levi.

Jasmine is amazed she can create anything
just by using the letters of the alphabet.
Next she writes the letter "B" and POOF!!!
...bubbles appear!
"BUBBLES!!!" screamed Levi. He loves the
way bubbles feel on his hands and face.

As Levi and Jasmine are playing with the bubbles they notice a little boy sitting by himself on the park bench. In the blink of an eye, they change back into their regular clothes.

Jasmine walks over to the boy and notices he had been crying. "What's wrong?" asked Jasmine.

"There's a kid in my class who makes fun of me because I wear my headphones and because I have Autism. Everytime I walk by him and his friends, they laugh at me, push me and call me weirdo."

"That's terrible!" said Jasmine.

Levi walks over to the boy and gives him a hug. "Aww what's wrong? Don't cry, it's okay."

Jasmine turned to the little boy and said, "We want to show you something." Jasmine took her magic glitter crayon and wrote "ABC" and POOF!!! She turned into ABC Girl!

"Hey Levi, where's your fidget spinner?" asked Jasmine. Levi didn't respond.

Jasmine drew the letter "F" and made a pic of a fidget spinner.

"OHHHH!!!" said Levi and pulled out his fidget spinner from his pocket.

He started spinning it and POOF!!! He turned into ECHO BOY.

"WOW!!! you both are super heroes?" said the boy.

"Yes we are" said Jasmine.

"YES WEEE ARE!!!" said Levi.

"I think it's time we talk to the bully and try to put an end to this," said Jasmine.

"I'm not so sure about that" said the boy. These kids are bigger than me and don't like me because I am different."

"Well my mom always told me that kids make fun of what they don't understand. Let's teach these kids about acceptance and kindness," said Jasmine.

"YAAAAAAY let's do it!!!" said Levi.

The following day the little boy saw his bullies at school and waited for the teasing. "I really hate coming to school" mumbled the little boy.

"Hey Michael!" yelled Jasmine. "HEY MICHAEL!!" repeated Levi. "Wait for us!" said Jasmine.

Suddenly for the first time in months, Michael didn't feel anxious or scared about going to school. He had the biggest smile on his face.

As they were walking to the school yard to line up, one of the bullies approached Michael, Levi and Jasmine.

"Hey weirdo! What's up? You wearing those stupid headphones again?" teased the bully.

Michael started getting upset and took out his fidget spinner to help with his anxiety.

"What is that?" said the bully and slapped it out of his hand.

Jasmine walked up to the bully and looked up at him and asked "Why do you like being mean to him?"

"Because he acts different and wears those headphones and he's not even listening to music."

"Well my mom always said if you can't say anything nice, don't say anything at all."

"Yeah, be nice!!" said Levi.

"Michael has Autism and even though he may see the world in a different way, that doesn't make him weird" said Jasmine.

"Whatever" said the bully and he walked away.

The bell started to ring, "Time for school!" said Levi.

"Michael how about you sit with me and Levi during lunch? Meet us by the cafeteria doors at 12:30" said Jasmine. "That sounds great!" said Michael.

All three kids had a pretty busy morning; Levi had speech therapy, Jasmine had an occupational therapy session and Michael was working on a project for the annual future leaders science fair.

12:30 came and Michael was waiting patiently at the cafeteria door for Levi and Jasmine.

Michael was playing with his fidget spinner when he looked up and saw the bully standing in front of him. The bully pushed Michael to the ground and started laughing at him. "LEAVE ME ALONE!" yelled Michael.

Meanwhile, Jasmine was helping Levi find his favorite toy car or else he was going to have a difficult time adjusting during lunch time.
They found the toy car and walked down the hallway and saw Michael crying on the floor. Standing in front of him was the bully and he dumped out his bookbag and found his lunch box. He took out his chocolate milk and poured it all over Michael while laughing.

Jasmine pulled Levi aside and said, "We need to help our friend!"
"Help our friend?" asked Levi.

"Yes!" said Jasmine.
She took out her magic glitter crayon and drew the letter "F" and made a picture of a fidget spinner. She showed Levi and immediately took out his fidget spinner and spun it 6 times and turned into ECHO BOY!

Jasmine wrote "ABC" and turned into ABC GIRL! "Okay, let's go help Michael and talk to this bully!" said Jasmine.

Echo Boy and ABC Girl approached the bully and Jasmine said, "Hey stop bullying Michael!"

"Oh yeah? And what are you gonna do about it?" said the bully.

Jasmine wrote the letter "A" and the word ACCEPTANCE appeared.

"This word means to acknowledge and understand another person for their differences."

"WE CAN BE FRIENDS!" said Levi.

"Bullying doesn't make you better than Michael" said Jasmine.

Levi looked into the bully's eyes and said, "he's sad."

Levi started spinning to calm his emotions and then said, "Love is the answer."

"What are you talking about?" said the bully.

"You are sad...You are soooooooo sad."

Levi kept repeating it over and over as he is clapping his hands.

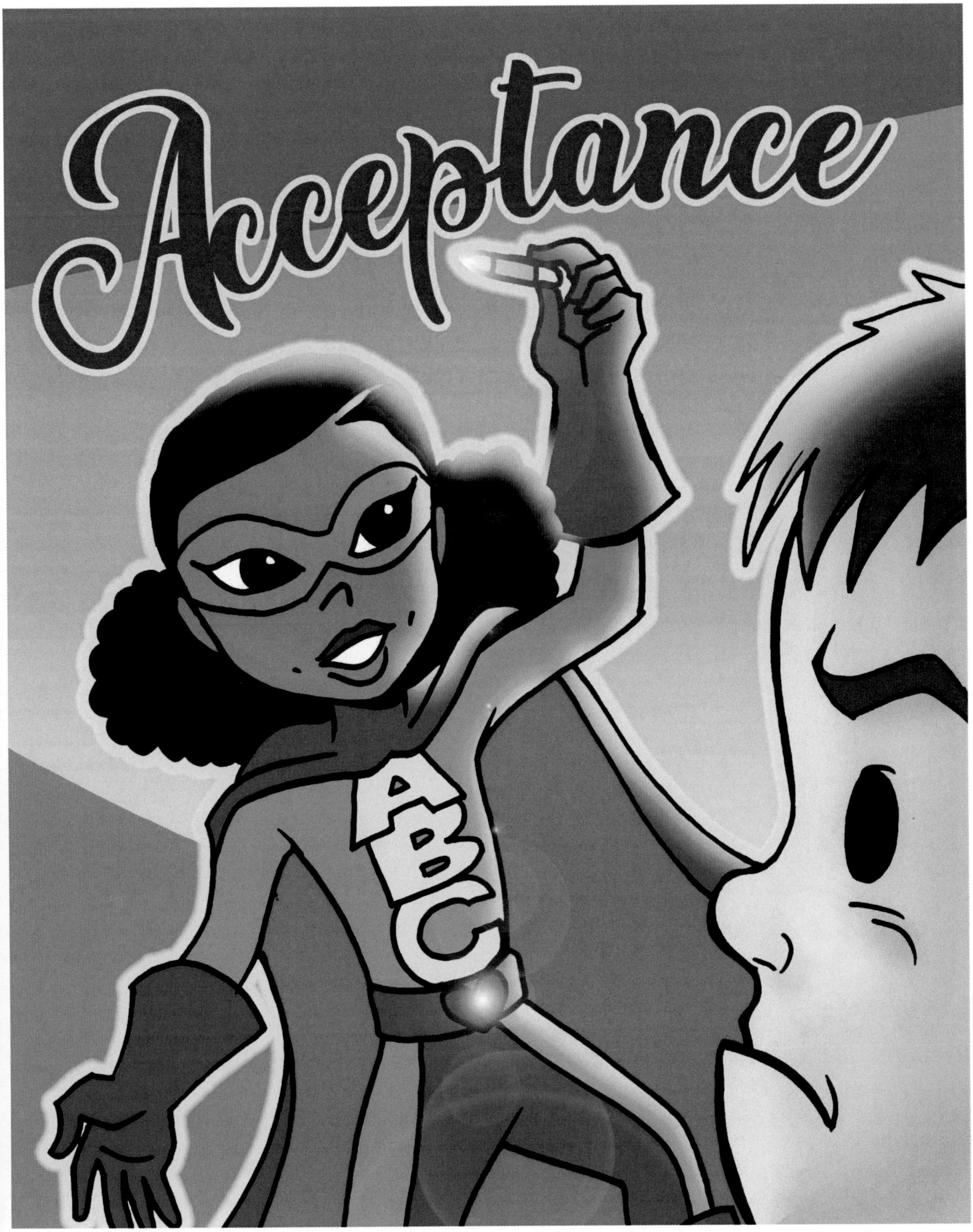
Acceptance
ABC

"Your parents got a divorce a year ago and your dad moved to another city." The bully was shocked that she knew that.

He finally opened up and started crying. "Yeah my parents got a divorce last year and my dad moved away. I miss him so much! I didn't know how to handle my feelings so I started making fun of Michael" said the bully.

"Well just because your dad moved away doesn't mean he stopped loving you. Bullying Michael isn't going to make the situation any better" said Jasmine. "Michael is an awesome kid and just wants to make friends. But ever since you started bullying him, he hates coming to school."

"Oh man I'm really sorry for all the mean things I said and did to you, Michael. Can you forgive me?" asked the bully.

Michael smiled and said "Yes I forgive you."

"What's your name?" asked Levi.

"My name is Brandon."

"Nice to meet you Brandon!" said Levi, Jasmine and Michael.

"Hey Michael! I'm gonna buy you lunch today since I took yours" Brandon said.

"That would be awesome!" said Michael.

"Brandon do you want to sit with us in the cafeteria?" asked Jasmine. "Yeah that would be great" said Brandon.

With a snap of the fingers, Echo Boy and ABC Girl turned back into Jasmine and Levi.

"I want a hot dog!" said Levi as he did a little happy dance. The rest of the kids laughed and walked to the cafeteria together as friends.

The End

Chante is a single parent of an amazing
6 year old boy named Levi.
They both reside in Philadelphia, PA.
Once she learned that her child was diagnosed
with Autism, she made it her priority to be
an advocate not just for her son, but for
all kids and adults.
Writing has always been her passion since
she was 16 years old.
Influenced by the love of superhero movies
and her son, Chante Douglas created
The Adventures of EchoBoy and ABC Girl.

Made in the USA
Middletown, DE
22 October 2021